Mended Fences

Brian J. Hill

CONTENTS

CHAPTER
1

Beep…Beep…Beep….

The monitor at the hospital keeping track of Jonathan's vital stats kept ringing in Meghan's ears long after walking down halls to the cafeteria. Even the bright, cheery walls with clowns and hot balloons painted on them in the children's wing couldn't alleviate her depression. Jonathan – or Johnny as Meghan affectionately called him – Meghan's ten year old brother, had been diagnosed with leukemia soon after birth. In and out of the hospital for years, the prognosis this time was looking grim. At twenty-five, Meghan had a tight bond with her brother. Since their dad had died in a car accident right before Jonathan was born, Meghan had usurped the parental role of helping their mother, Jennifer, to raise Jonathan. Though a few men had expressed interest in Jennifer, when they found out that she had a son who required constant medical attention, they had rarely called after the first dinner date. Meghan, too, had not found "Mr. Right" either. Most men she had met were either egotistical young businessmen who liked to talk about their trust funds, their developing 401ks, or their business deals requiring them to blur the lines between career advancement and dishonesty; some she met were still "discovering themselves" and hoping to find women to support them. Most didn't see the value that having a friendship before a relationship could bring to the relationship. Being brought up in a Christian household, she was not going to just settle for any man who happened to come along just so she could have a man. She had learned early on that just because they looked good on the outside didn't mean that they were equally good on the inside. Just because they could provide financial stability didn't mean that they could provide good emotional and spiritual stability. She wanted to find a man who could share her values and dreams and someone who would value her for being her.

"Oops! Sorry!" Meghan nearly collided with a nurse coming around the corner, causing her roaming thoughts to come to an end as she entered the cafeteria. There sat her mom, eyes swollen, sipping from a small Styrofoam cup of coffee.

"It's not quite Starbucks is it, Mom?"

"Not even close."

"Did you get any sleep last night?"

"Just a couple of hours at most. I don't know why it's so hard this time."

"It's because of the decision that you and Johnny made. This time there is a game plan."

"I know. His oncologist, Dr. Weaver, agrees that it is probably the best for him. I thought I had come to terms with it, too. But he's my son. I just can't bring myself to think about losing him."

"Yeah, and he's my little brother. I fed him; I changed his diapers; I don't want to let go. I just put it out of my mind, and then all of the sudden, I break down, too. I had to lose Dad; do I have to lose him, too?"

"I know, honey, it's tough."

"Jennifer, Meghan, Dr. Weaver's just come in. I thought you might want to catch him."

"Thanks, Delores. I don't know what we would do without you."

Delores, a middle aged nurse who had been with the hospital since Jonathan had been born, was almost like a part of their family. She was more than just a nurse – she was a friend, a confidant, a comforter. Jennifer and Meghan also lived vicariously through Delores' stories about her family. They knew about her eldest son, Tyrell, who with his wife had just given Delores a great gift – a grandson. They also knew about Jerome, Delores' younger son, who was nearly finished with his college degree, a B.S. in Business Management.

"Dr. Weaver, what can you tell us?" Jennifer asked.

"Well, I still think our plan should be what we initially decided. There are some traditional treatment methods, like chemo and radiation, that we still can continue, but we have pretty much exhausted the possibilities of those continuing to work after almost nine years. There are some more radical, alternative treatment methods we can still pursue, but if they will really help him is really a very iffy situation. They will make him really sick, and they will help sustain life a little longer, but not cure him. Plus, they are very expensive, and the insurance usually doesn't cover them. Another option, of course, is a transplant, but it is questionable if it will even help, and we have to find a donor. Due to the worry that it might not work and due to cost issues, the insurance is refusing to pay for it, even though I have stressed to them that it is a medical necessity. The other option, of course, is to do what we reasonably can, keep him comfortable, and let nature take its course."

With tears welling in her eyes, Jennifer replied, "Well, we sat down and talked some more about this as a family – explaining everything to Johnny – and he said that he didn't want to be sick and hurt anymore. He understood that like the past treatments, new ones will really affect him, so he wants comfort. He understands that a transplant might help, but it is very questionable. Please understand that I'm not worried about the expense. We'll make it happen somehow. That is not the problem. You know some parents will fight to the end for their child's life – at any cost – no matter how painful to the child, but I know that sometimes things don't work out the way you would like for them to, and you have to do what is best for the child. It doesn't make it any easier, though. I just want to thank you for your support and laying out all of our options. I'm so glad that you agree with our decision."

"I know, and I am so sorry. I still think you all are doing the right thing, though. Let Jonathan enjoy life to the fullest. I am going to send Jonathan home today. If he becomes significantly ill, bring him back to the ER. However, when the time comes, which it will soon, I am going to call in hospice for you all."

"Again, thank you for all you have done, Dr. Weaver."

"Yes, Dr. Weaver, thank you for all you have done for my brother."

That night, after tucking Jonathan in, Meghan came in to the kitchen to find her mother, her head resting in hands, bent over her checkbook with a pile of opened and unopened envelopes surrounding her, eyes red and swollen again.

"Mom, are we doing okay?"

"Honey, I am going to be honest with you – no, not very well. Your father and my little bit of savings is long gone. His life insurance money is almost spent, too. The insurance company is refusing to pay as much as possible – stating that providers are out of network or a certain procedure is not covered or not necessary. I am able to make a little selling crafts online, but not what we need. You know I have to be available almost 24/7 in case there is an emergency, and of course I am homeschooling Johnny because he just can't attend public school with all of his health problems. I can't thank you enough for the sacrifices you've made – taking a college class or two at a time, postponing your dream of becoming a vet, moving back home, donating your income for bills every week, living economically, basically putting your life on hold. It's so unfair to you."

"But Mom, I wanted to," Meghan said running her hand through her shoulder-length, wavy honey blonde hair, "or I wouldn't have done it."

"Your dad had a good job, made good money, and we had good investments. However, after the car accident..." Jennifer's voice trailed off. "He was a good provider, and when we were first married, I worked because I wanted to. Working for the florist had the advantage of a flexible schedule when you eventually came along. I could take you to school and be home for you when you came home. I could be there for the important

8

school things, and I could take you to work with me during the summer. I am lucky to have been able to stay at home with Jonathan since he was diagnosed at only a year old. I really shouldn't even say lucky – we didn't have any choice with all of the doctor appointments and hospital stays." She brushed her hair back with both of her hands and pulled it into a ponytail. She looked quite similar in build to Meghan – around 5'4 with hair similar in color to Meghan's except for the gray streaks, which seemed more prominent now than before. Her bright blue eyes were also similar to Meghan's except that they had seemed to dull with age and stress. Their slender builds could be credited in part to the loving to be outside and active and in part to barely eating over the last few months - stress that life had provided with Jonathan's diagnosis and intensified with the most recent developments. "You deserve something nice, someone nice, too."

"Don't worry about me. I want you to know, though, that I'm going to try to do something really special for Johnny. I am going to do a little researching, and then I'll probably have to take a little road trip," Meghan announced.

"What are you going to do?"

"You'll just have to wait and see," Meghan replied with a twinkle in her eye.

CHAPTER
2

"Now, let's see about this." Meghan was sitting in a comfortably upholstered chair in the college student commons area. She had connected to the college's Wi-Fi and was performing an internet search on Johnny's hero, Jared "Bronc Buster" Cochran. She knew that Jared didn't ride the circuits anymore, and she remembered that there was some sort of scandal. The judge had found him innocent of all charges during the main trial, but his career had ended abruptly. Regardless, he was still the focus of Johnny's admiration. Johnny had Jared's posters on his walls, action figures in his toy box, tons of his books on his shelves, and several of his movies featuring his rodeo archives. Meghan learned from her online search that he had made quite a bit of money and had definitely reached celebrity status, but he always had declined the limelight. He was always pretty much a recluse but even more so since his departure from the circuit. She found that he lived about five hours away in northwestern Missouri. She realized that from central Missouri it wasn't too far of a drive, especially when it was concerning something for her little brother.

Classes and her part time job had worked out so that she had an extended weekend coming up. Meghan had already packed a change of clothes and toiletries. After researching and finding what she needed, with the extra time on hand, Meghan left the student commons, jumped in her blue Ford Ranger and took off on a five hour drive.

Once she arrived in the town where Jared was supposed to live, she realized that she really didn't have much of a plan. After driving around for a bit, she noticed a rodeo themed bar and grill. She parked and went in. She could see a thick cloud of cigarette smoke hanging in the air and immediately began coughing and wondering if this hadn't been such a good idea.

"Sorry, we don't serve minors, babe," said the bartender, a man with a scruffy, long gray beard and an equally long gray ponytail with a red bandana wrapped around his head.

"First, I'm over 21, but thanks for the compliment. Second, I am looking for someone."

"Aren't we all," smiled the bartender.

"I read that Jared 'Bronc Buster' Cochran lives around here. However, he's pretty elusive. I wondered if you could tell me where I might be able to find him."

"J doesn't come in here very often. He's pretty much a hermit anymore since the incident. We all know him, though. He lives a few miles outside of town. Take this road in front of the bar here, make a left, and then get back on the Interstate. Go north. That will take you out of town. It's about 15 minutes up the road. Take the County Road A exit. Make a left. Go over the overpass, and make a right. Make a left on the next gravel road. Follow that for about four miles, and you'll see his place. His is the ranch on the left. It has a sign that says 'Circle C Ranch.'"

"I think I got it," Meghan said, frantically writing the directions on the back of the receipt she had from when she last filled up her gas tank. "Thanks so much!"

"No problem-o. I told you where he lives. But I didn't say he liked company."

"I'll worry about that when I get there. Thanks again."

"Wow, this is beautiful!" Meghan exclaimed when she pulled close to what she presumed was Jared Cochran's house. It was a nice half brick and half freshly painted white wooden ranch-style house with sprawling acreage fenced in some areas with white wooden boards and other areas with barbed wire. There were cattle roaming within some of the fence and horses within some of the other. It looked like the owner took pride in keeping the estate well kept. She parked and headed up toward the house.

"Hold it right there." She looked and a man in a cowboy hat had rounded the corner of the house with a sawed off shotgun pointed right at her. "Whatever it is, I already have one or don't need it since I lived this long without it already. Get in your vehicle and go," the man gruffly said.

All of the sudden, tears burst from Meghan's eyes. She thought that she had gotten past the point of grief where unexpected tears flowed freely. "Please don't shoot me."

The man put down his gun and took a few steps closer. The angry look on his face melted away to one of compassion. "I'm sorry; I didn't mean to scare you. I just don't like company or reporters coming around, though I don't have much of them anymore. Sometimes somebody doing a senior thesis needs an interview or something."

"No, it's just...I shouldn't have come out here, but I didn't know how else to get in touch with you.... The man at the bar said you lived out this way.... I drove all the way here to meet you and get a picture of you for my little brother who has cancer really bad and is gonna die soon, and.... I just...."

"It's okay. Let me put my shotgun away. Sit down. I'll be right back."

Meghan sat down in a wicker chair on the porch. Wiping the tears from her eyes, she noticed that the man coming back to sit with her really was Jared "Bronc Buster" Cochran. She could see his features more clearly without his cowboy hat. At about 5'10, with thinning brownish graying hair and beginning of wrinkles around his eyes, he looked older than he appeared in Johnnie's posters. Even at around 50 years old, though, he was still extremely handsome.

"Now, what can I do for you?"

"Well," Meghan said, clearing her throat, "Mr. Cochran, I am Meghan Schulte. My brother who is ten years old is dying of cancer. He adores you. He is probably your biggest fan." Meghan wiped tears from her eyes. "He thinks the world of you. I am sure that you are asked all of the time for autographs or to have pictures taken with you, so I hate to ask. But, I wondered if I could take a picture of you and have you autograph this picture for him? It would mean the world to him. My mom doesn't have much money and we really can't afford gifts right now, but this would be the best present he could ever get for his upcoming birthday." She pulled out a folded magazine article of Jared from her purse.

"Well, first of all, call me J. It's what all of my friends call me. Sure, I'll be happy to give an autograph and take a picture." He took the magazine article from Meghan's hand, unfolded, looked at it and smiled. Meghan realized that he was still very, very handsome when he smiled. "Let me see if I can do a little better." Jared handed her back the page and went back into the house; soon he came back out with an eight by ten professionally taken photograph. "I used to autograph these back in the day," Jared said as he signed the picture. "What is your brother's name?"

"Johnny"

"All right," J said scribbling a message with his marker. "Sorry it took a couple of minutes. I had to find the box where they were stored and wipe the inches of dust from it. "

She grinned and said, "I hardly think that you had dust collecting on your pictures."

"You never know," J replied as he handed her the autographed picture.

"Let's take a picture of both of us so that he knows that you're telling the truth when you say that you met me!"

She grabbed her phone, leaned next to J, delighting in the intoxication of his after shave, and snapped a picture of them together.

"There! Proof! Now you said that you drove all the way here just to get an autograph and picture? Where do you live anyway?"

Meghan explained how she lived almost five hours away.

"Well, he must really be a special little boy."

"He is. He's my whole life." She scrolled through the pictures on her phone and showed a few to Jared. "I just wish I could do more for him or even trade places with him. I love him so much. I've helped my mom to raise him, and well.... Sorry, I'm rambling. It's just that I can't believe that I got to meet you and am actually sitting her talking to you. You're a celebrity, but you seem so down to earth, so common. My brother, Johnny, has admired you since he was old enough to know what a rodeo is. He had really wanted to see you ride in a rodeo and eventually grow up to be in a rodeo himself. Well, you left the circuit, and he probably won't live long enough to ever grow up to be in a rodeo.... Here I am rambling again." Meghan noticed that she was nervously picking at a small hole in her jeans. "Well, I've taken up enough of your time. How much do I owe you for the picture?"

"Not a thing. Tell him that J says that he's a courageous young man and to hang in there. I'll be praying for you all...." There was a pause in the conversation.

"Well, thank you so much." Meghan hesitated, "I can't tell you how much this means to me and to him. Well, I had better get going."

"Yeah, you have quite a long drive back."

"I'm staying in town tonight so that I can get up early and make the drive back.... Well, bye and thanks again!"

Meghan noticed that there had seemed to be tears welling up in Jared's eyes as she had talked about Jonathan and then as Jared waved goodbye to her.

"Knock...knock...knock...."

Meghan looked at the clock. 9:30 PM.

"Knock...knock...knock...."

"What in the world?" Megan heard the knocking again on her motel room door. Nobody knew she was here. The television wasn't too loud, so nobody should have complained. She put down her cell phone, pausing from checking her social media accounts, then thinking better of it, picked it up again in case she needed to dial 911, and went to the door. She peaked out the small hole in the door and saw...Jared Cochran standing there. He was still in his western flannel shirt, jeans, work boots, and again, a cowboy hat.

She opened the door. "Mr. Cochran?" she questioned, pulling her light robe around her t-shirt and pajama pants.

"Yes, I'm sorry to bother you so late but I got to thinking about something." Jared shuffled the toe of his book on the concrete sidewalk outside of the motel room door.

"Yes...?"

"You said that your brother always dreamed of being in a rodeo?"

"Yes...."

"Well, I got to thinking about it. I realize how much riding has meant to me, and then I got to feeling really bad for your brother. If you all would approve of it, I think I can arrange special, comfortable transportation for him to come up here and spend a few days at least learning how to ride a little. It might kind of help fulfill his dream. Since the long trip is rather long, I have the perfect vehicle for him to travel in. Of course, I'm not saying that your truck wouldn't be comfortable," Jared said while glancing over at the small pickup. He then glanced back down into her bright blue eyes. "And I want you and your mom to come up, too."

"Uh, how did you find me?" was the only thing that she could manage to respond.

"I knew you said that you were going to stay in town. The motels are pretty limited, plus, remember, I've got connections around here."

"...uh, that's right. I did say that. I'm sorry; I was just so surprised. Do you really mean that you will teach my brother how to ride, and you're going to transport him here? I mean, we don't have much money to pay you for transportation or for riding lessons and we sure don't have a horse."

"That's alright. I've thought a lot about what you've said today, and like I said, I feel so sorry for you and your brother.

Sometimes when you donate money to different organizations that are supposed to help people, you really wonder how much of it actually gets there to help. So I try to help in small ways, ways that I can see will actually benefit real people with real needs. Yours is a real need. There's no cost. It's just something I can do to try to be nice, to help. Plus, I do have a horse and riding area."

"Let me talk to Mom and Johnny, but that should work. In fact, it sounds really awesome! I didn't expect this at all. I thought I would be doing good just to get an autograph and picture."

"Great! Here is my phone number," Jared said while handing her a slip of paper. "Let me know if it is all right and when you all can come up."

"Do you have a cell phone?"

"Yes...."

"Here, let me have it." She quickly punched her phone number into his contact list. "This is how we do this these days."

"Well, what if my phone dies?"

"You better hope it doesn't...." She replied with a mischievous smile. "Otherwise, you'll have to send your carrier pigeon."

"Right...well it is past this old man's bed time. Better get going. Talk to you soon!"

They waved goodbye and after shutting the door, Meghan leaned against its wooden frame. Was this really happening? Had she actually gotten up the nerve to go to Jared "Bronc Buster" Cochran's place? Had she just flirted a little with him? Was she going to get to see him again?

Meghan couldn't have been happier as she pulled the sheet up around her neck. Even if it was an old, hard motel pillow, her head felt like it was floating on a cloud.

CHAPTER
3

"Knock, knock," Meghan lightly tapped on Johnny's door.

"Hey, Sis!"

"Hey, Buddy!"

"Where've you been? I've missed you?"

"Well, I had an errand to do. Aren't you going to ask if I brought you anything?"

"Gee, Meggie, I'm not a little kid anymore!"

"Yes, but you'll always be my little brother, and your favorite sister did bring you something."

"You're my only sister…,but whatcha got?"

"You're never going to believe who I met yesterday!"

"Who?"

She ran her hand over the poster of Jared "Bronc Buster" Cochran hanging on Johnny's wall.

"What, you got to meet him? Where? No way!" Johnny's huge grin dropped to a frown. "You got to meet him, and I didn't. It isn't fair! You don't even like him!"

"That is where you are wrong," Meghan thought to herself as she remembered those beautiful brown eyes that had looked into hers just yesterday. "Well, since I've heard that you've been such a good boy, I have a couple of surprises for you."

"Yes…!"

She pulled out the autographed picture that she had received yesterday.

"Whoa…."

"I went to Jared Cochran's ranch to try to get an autograph for you. But here's more. Jared would like to meet you. He thinks you've been a really brave guy, and he has invited us to spend some time on his ranch. He's going to teach you how to ride."

Johnny just sat there with his mouth open and eyes wide. He was not only going to get to meet his hero. His hero was going to teach him how to ride!

"Is Mom really gonna let me go?"

"Yes, she is!"

Meghan remembered talking to their mom about it. How her mom had been unsure about it at first. What if Johnny got hurt learning to ride? However, she realized what it would mean to Johnny and really, what did he have to lose at this point? After a quick phone call to his doctor, Jennifer gave her approval. When Meghan called Jared to make the arrangements, he had answered on the first ring.

"We can come up next Thursday if you still want us to."

"Yes.... Great! I'll arrange for transportation to arrive for you all that day. I'll call you later this week to arrange the details."

"Thanks so much for doing this for Johnny."

"No problem!"

"See you Thursday," Meghan said.

"It's a date."

"It sure is," she whispered after the click.

CHAPTER
4

Thursday couldn't come soon enough for Johnny or Meghan either for that matter. She had spent all week trying to decide what outfits she should take. Dresses? Heels? Jeans? Boots? Dress to impress or for comfort? Undoubtedly Jared had been around a lot of beautiful women in his career. Was he married? Did he have a girlfriend? Would he even look at her as she was beginning to look at him? That cute smile as he turned to look at you. That tall, lean build. What had begun as a mission to do something special for her brother was beginning to take a different turn. She had crushed on some guys before, but she was beginning to fall hard. The ironic part? Jared "Bronc Buster" Cochran posters had adorned the walls around her for years. Her bare feet had stepped on his action figures countless times as she walked in to check on her brother over the years. Why hadn't she noticed how handsome the man really was?

She was just slipping on her sandals when she heard the doorbell ring downstairs.

"Yea! He's here!" screamed Johnny, running down the stairs to open the door.

As Meghan came down the stairs, she saw a tall, lanky, slightly hunched over cowboy with a white handlebar mustache that matched the white hair sticking out from under his large cowboy hat picking up luggage that had been thoughtfully packed throughout the week. He looked to rather old, but the gleam in his eye reminded her of a small child at Christmas.

"You must be Miss Meghan," the older gentleman said, sticking his hand out to Jennifer to had just come in from the kitchen.

"No, actually I'm her mother, Jennifer."

"Well, I declare! J...Jared, but everyone calls him J... said I was to pick up a pretty young lady with some young feller who was her body guard. I assumed you were her. Besides you don't look old enough to have a daughter in her 20's."

Jennifer was blushing as she shook the man's hand. Meghan's face was completely red. "A pretty young lady" was how Jared had described her to this older man. "Wow!"

"My name's Sidney Tellerman, but folks just calls me Sid. It's nice to make your acquaintance, ma'am."

As Sid then introduced himself to her, Meghan couldn't help but like him. He had such a folksy appeal and his voice sounded like someone from one of the western movies or television shows she had seen on rerun channels. She then stepped outside and saw what was waiting for them – a black limousine.

"Wow!" Johnny went running out the door, past her and jumped into the opened car door. He began feeling the upholstered seats. "Where's Jared?"

"Well, Young Buckaroo, Jared's back at his house, finishing up his chores. He sent me to pick y'all up. If you get tired and sleepy along the way, this here limo's got reclining seats so that you can stay buckled up but also recline and maybe even watch a little tv."

"Wow, there's a tv in there, too?"

"Yep, and one of those dvd players, too. I've got the whole *Gunsmoke* series on dvd, a few John Wayne movies, and a few other titles you might enjoy a little better!"

"Wow! Do you have some movies with Jared in them? Wait...you said Jared is doing his chores right now. You really mean Jared's got chores to do? And this limo's really for us?"

"Yes, and yes. Gotta do his chores so that the animals get fed and watered. Don't want 'em going hungry. You just remember that when you try to get outta your chores at home, too! There's some cola and root beer back there in mini fridge, too. There's some snacks back there, too. You know, you must be an all right feller seein' how he sent this here limo up especially for you, young buckaroo."

They finished loading the limo and started a movie to watch on the way; as they began the trip, Sid called Jared to let him know that they were heading out.

They traveled the five hour distance, stopping only two or three times for bathroom breaks. Sid kept a constant stream of conversation going with Jennifer the entire time.

When they eventually pulled up the lane, a large black and white border collie came running down the gravel lane, barking and then chasing the car back to the house. When they pulled up near the front door, Sid parked, jumped out, and then opened the limo door so that the occupants could exit. The collie was wagging his tail and jumping on everyone as they exited the limo.

Johnny, fresh from a nap, jumped out of the limo. When he saw Jared making his way from the barn to the car, he began running as fast as he could toward Jared with his arms outstretched. After a hug that seemed to never end, Johnny pulled away and said, "I can't believe it's actually you. I've always wanted to meet you. I have all your movies and all your books and all your action figures, and all your posters, and all...."

"He gets the point," Jennifer said, approaching with her hand outstretched. "I'm Jennifer, the mom to these two crazy kids. Thank you so much for inviting us."

"Yes, thank you so much!" chimed in Johnny.

"Hi, J," Meghan said as she stepped forward. She quickly put her arms around him, giving him a quick hug, but lingering long enough to again savor the smell of his after shave lotion.

"What are we gonna do first?" Johnny cried.

"Well, first we need to get you all settled in your rooms. Come on in when you're ready," Sid spoke up, picking up several pieces of luggage, balancing them every way possible in his arms.

Jennifer followed Sid inside, helping to carry some of the luggage, but Johnny couldn't tear himself away from Jared. He kept staring up at Jared with intense admiration, taking in every little detail of this current moment in his life.

As Jared took Johnny to the barn to start showing him around the farm, Meghan wandered into the house. When she rounded the corner into the kitchen, she came face to face with a pretty, slim blonde who looked to be in her late thirties or early forties.

"Oh, sorry," Meghan said, almost knocking the mystery woman over. Her face started to flush, with embarrassment for her blunder, but also for letting herself think that this seemingly perfect man would still be on the market. She knew that even with her trim figure, she could present no competition with this beautiful, young woman.

"No problem. You must be Meghan. Jared's said quite a lot about you."

"He has a gorgeous woman here, and he's talking about me. He must be trying to make her jealous or something. Wait, I'm talking like I even had a chance. He didn't actually give me any inclination that he was available or even interested in me. He must be a really smooth ladies' man. Great, I'm stuck here for a few days as a fifth wheel – how embarrassing."

"Are you okay," the blonde said interrupting Meghan's train of thoughts.

"Yeah, sorry, I was just thinking about something," Meghan replied. She noticed that her own expression had already fallen into one of depression. "I've got to spend all this time here now with his wife. It's hard not to be jealous," she now thought.

"My name is Sara. I'm Jared's sister," she heard the blonde saying.

"Wait, you're his sister?"

"Yep, I'm several years younger than Jared is. He's always looked out for me."

A rush of relief cascaded through Meghan. "Well, it's nice to meet you. Well, I guess that I had better go find my room."

"Sure! We'll have some more time to visit later on."

Meghan quickly turned the corner, feeling her smile beginning to return and found her mother and Sid, grinning from

22

ear to ear under his mustache, walking down the hall toward the front door.

"Sid's showed me around the house and now he's gonna show me around the grounds. He's such a fun guy!" Jennifer giggled with delight.

"Yes and your room is down the hall, second door on the right. I put your suitcases in there already," Sid said.

Meghan sat down in a chair in her room to rest for a while, and when she opened her eyes again, she saw that it was pretty much dark outside. She came down the hall and into the family room area. There she saw her mom halfway watching some reality show on television while lightly chuckling, listening to Sid tell wild tales to Johnny while the two played marbles.

"You mean you really fought at the Alamo?" Johnny's eyes were wide with excitement.

"Yessirree. Me and ole Davy Crocket would shoot at them ornery fellers for a while, and then sit back, drink a little root beer and play a little cards. Then, we'd get back up and shoot at 'em a little more.... Now when the Civil War came around, ole Ulysses S. Grant, hisself, knocked on my door and says to me, 'Sid, I want you to grab them there muskets and charge over that hill there.'"

Meghan had to smile to herself. She walked around by another room that seemed like an office. Here she saw Jared and Sara looking over what appeared to be some important papers. They were frowning, and Jared said, "Well, I'll call Larry about this in the morning. Maybe he'll have an update." The border collie, laying against Jared's foot, looked up and wagged his tail at Meghan.

Meghan walked through the kitchen, where she stopped and took a diet soft drink from the refrigerator. She made her way out the patio door and saw a boy about Johnny's age sitting out on a patio chair, playing a game on his phone.

"Oh, hi! You must be Meghan!" the boy said.

"Does everyone around here know who I am?" wondered Meghan. "Yes, I am," she replied.

"Cool. J's talked a lot about you. I'm Tyler; Sara's my mom. I met Johnny earlier. He's really cool."

Meghan sat and visited with Tyler for a while, enjoying the nice evening breeze. She found out that Tyler's dad had left him and his mom a few years ago after an affair with a co-worker. Tyler's dad was looking to mend his relationship with his son. He wanted to spend more time with Tyler now. While Jennifer had to home school Johnny due to his health, Tyler, who was in fifth grade at the local elementary school, had told Johnny earlier of the joys to behold at public school. He really enjoyed school, so the past absence of his dad was not so painful with something enjoyable to fill his time. It was great that the two young boys, so different, still had so much in common. While Tyler was enjoying his summer break, he was looking forward to going into a new building for middle school. At least he had that to anticipate. After visiting for a while longer, Meghan went back inside to her room and fell fast asleep.

CHAPTER
5

"Rise and shine, all you young buckaroos!" Sid bellowed, walking up and down the hall while clanging on a metal pan with a metal spoon. "The flapjacks are almost ready!"

Meghan groggily sat up, wiping the blurriness from her eyes. What time was it anyway? She glanced at the clock beside her. 9:00 AM. How could she have slept so long?

Johnny came bounding in, jumping on her bed. "Come on, Sis. Sid and I have been up since the crack of dawn working on breakfast for y'all."

"Oh boy," thought Meghan, "he's already starting to sound like Sid."

Meghan ran into her bathroom, prepared for the day, and headed to the kitchen. Everyone but Jared was already at the breakfast table.

"Hello, Sleepy Head," Jennifer teased.

Meghan sat down to the already set breakfast table. After blessing the food, everyone dug in. Meghan took a scoop of scrambled eggs and a pancake. She finally was able to get the bottle of syrup after Johnny who had already drenched his three pancakes with it.

"Well, I see that your appetite seems to be returning nicely," Meghan said.

"Yea, Sid said that all the nice, fresh, country air would help me feel better. I think maybe some of my hair is beginning to come back, too." Johnny felt protectively of his bald head, the effects of the chemotherapy. "But I still think I'll wear my cowboy hat just like J."

"Speaking of J, where is he?" Meghan inquired.

"I'm right here," Jared said while coming in the door.

Johnny jumped up and ran around to give him a hug. "We

saved you the best pancakes. Sid and I worked all morning making them."

"Thanks! They'll be good, then. I had to check on some of the fence in the northern pasture. Sid, it looks like we're gonna need to work on that barbed wire a little."

"That barbed wire isn't going to go anywhere," Sid said playfully.

"Yeah, but the cattle might," Jared kidded back.

"J, can you teach me how to fix barbed wire?" Johnny asked.

"Sure, if it's alright with your mom. There is nothing more satisfying to see than a mended fence. "

"Please, mom! Please! Please!"

"Okay."

After breakfast, Jared announced that he was going into town and asked if anyone wanted to go to.

"Me! Me!" Johnny exclaimed.

"All right, do you want to go, too?" Jared asked, looking at Meghan.

"Sure!"

After the table was cleared, Jennifer and Sara began the dishes, Tyler went with Sid outside to check on the north pasture, and Jared, Meghan, and Johnny got in Jared's shiny, red pickup. Johnny, sitting between Jared and Meghan, ran his hands over the slick upholstery.

"Wow, when I get to be sixteen, I want a truck just like this!" Johnny exclaimed. Then his expression dropped and looking down, he said, "That is, if I get to be sixteen."

"Well, Johnny, we've all got to live life every day to the fullest. None of us know how many days we have left here on earth."

Jared parked right in front of an old-time looking drug store on the town square. He pulled out a twenty dollar bill and handed it to Meghan. "I have something I have to take care of, so why don't you all wait for me in there. They still have fountain drinks, homemade ice cream, and some of the best licorice around."

As they parted ways, Meghan couldn't help but look back at Jared, his confident walk, his pleasant demeanor. She also couldn't help but notice that the sign above the door he went in read, "Larry Posner, Attorney at Law."

"Come on, sis, I'm thirsty," Johnny whined, tugging at her arm.

After about forty five minutes, Jared sauntered into the store and plopped up on a stool at the counter next to Meghan. "Sorry about it taking so long," Jared said.

"No problem. Thanks for taking us along...and for the treats here!"

Johnny was off to the side playing pinball on an old fashioned looking machine.

"I won! I won!" They both heard him scream.

"So what exactly do you do?" Jared asked Meghan.

"Well, I take college classes as I can. I also work part time at a veterinarian's office. I am studying to be a vet. I used to live in an apartment in the city where I worked full and went to school full time. However, after dad died in the car wreck and Johnny kept getting sicker and sicker, it got to be too much for Mom to take care of by herself. I eventually moved back to help her with Johnny and to bundle our income to help with medical expenses. The part-time job allows me to have flexibility to help Mom with Johnny and take classes as I can."

"You all have been through a lot."

"They figure Johnny will last around six months, give or take. If he could get a transplant that might buy him a little time, but the insurance won't approve it. Oh, they might pay a tiny bit, but nothing substantial. What you've done for Johnny in letting him come up here – that's been tremendous. He's always had a positive outside in spite of everything, but I haven't seen him this happy since...I don't know when."

"Hey, guys, did you see me? Huh, did you see me?" Johnny had run over and was tugging on both of their arms.

"Yes, we did. Hey, are you about ready to go see how to fix barbed wire fence?" Meghan couldn't help but smile at Jared as he asked Johnny about the fence. Jared was so good with Johnny, and with his nephew Tyler, that she couldn't help but wonder why Jared had never become a father himself.

The afternoon and evening were full of pleasant fun. After coming in from fixing fence with Sid, Tyler, and Johnny, Jared fired up the grill. With the help of Sara and Jennifer, Meghan quickly whipped up a fresh green salad and brought out the potato chips and drinks. She knew that she had never had such good hamburgers and hot dogs before in her life.

The next morning, Meghan rose early; she had remembered to set the clock the night before. She snuck downstairs and began raiding the refrigerator and cabinets, looking for breakfast items. She began a pot of coffee and started cracking eggs to scramble. She glanced up and saw Jared standing there, watching her. It was obvious that he had been up for a while. Clean shaven, with a new looking Wrangler shirt and pressed blue jeans, he was definitely ready to meet the day.

"You're up early today. You're also stealing Sid's job," Jared joked. As he came closer, she could smell the fresh after shave that intoxicated her every time. Though ready for the day, she could see that his eyes seemed tired and seemed to bear the stress that the rest of his body seemed to hide.

"I think Sid will be okay," Meghan replied mischievously.

"Say, since I've caught you, I uh...well, I'm not very good at this...."

"Yes...."

"Well, tonight is Saturday night. In town, they always have country line and swing dancing, and the best food in town, and well, you have sacrificed so much – putting your dreams on hold to help with your brother – I just thought that you needed a night out on the town."

"Are you asking me out?"

"Yes, I guess that I am."

"Well, I'm not the best dancer, but I enjoy getting out there and making a fool of myself anyway. Sure! I'd love to go!"

She couldn't believe that Jared "Bronc Buster" Cochran – the Jared "Bronc Buster" Cochran – had just asked her out on a date.

Breakfast finally consisted of scrambled eggs, bagels with cream cheese, fruit, juice, and coffee. Meghan was so excited, looking forward to that evening, that she barely heard all of the compliments concerning her cooking.

After breakfast, Meghan retired to her room to select the perfect outfit and accessories for her date. She couldn't believe that Jared had asked her out. It was so surreal! Jared had taken Johnny out to the field near the barn and was showing him how to ride. He had a small pony that was very gentle and exactly the size Johnny needed. Pretty soon, looking out her window, Meghan could see Jared on his horse, leading Johnny on the pony alongside him. She couldn't help but smile, first at how good Jared was with Johnny, and second, at their upcoming date. She hadn't dated in a while, so she was really excited about that evening.

Johnny eventually had to go inside and rest after riding for a while. Jared, in turn, went to the north pasture to work before having to come in and clean up. Eventually, Sid rode out to the north pasture to help, and saw Jared's ATV parked along the fence line. The toolbox was wide open, but Jared was nowhere to be seen. Sid rode on up the fence row, over the slight hill, and saw Jared sitting still on the ground, with his eyes closed and back resting against the metal post.

"You okay?" Sid jumped off his horse and tied the reigns to the post.

"Oh, yeah, I just got really tired and thought I'd rest for a bit. I guess I kind of dozed off."

"Need me to take you to the doctor?"

"No, I got it. You know we're just under a lot of stress. I just let it get to me."

"Don't let it bother you. You know we've always gotten through all of this before. We can again."

"I know. I went in and talked to Larry today. He's fully aware of the situation and working on it."

"Well, let's get you back to the house to rest and get cleaned up a bit. I understand that you got a big date ahead of you tonight. I'll finish up this repair work later on."

They packed up and made their way back to the house.

Meghan and Sara came down the hall, and Sara stepped into the kitchen where most everyone else was sitting, saying, "Now presenting a true cowgirl... Miss Meghan."

Meghan stepped in the kitchen wearing a sparkly top with a jean skirt and cowgirl boots. Her hair was styled and in an up do. Her face, usually adorned with light traces of make-up and blush, had the look of professional glamor application.

"Woah, sis, you look weird!"

Jared walked in from outside and stopped in his tracks, staring.

"You two head on out now," Sid said. "Miss Jennifer is going to show me how to make one of her delicious peach cobblers that I've been hearing so much about. I'm the official taster. We gotta whole bunch of ice cream that's got my name on it; it'll go great with that cobbler. The boys got some kinda game they want to play on their phones, and Sara's got some work to do in the office. We all got stuff we've got to do, so get on now!"

Jared opened the passenger door for Meghan and helped her into the pickup. He went around, got in, put the key in the ignition and started the truck. Meghan scooted over to the middle so that she was sitting right next to Jared. She looked up at him and smiled.

They pulled up to the roadhouse; as soon as they got out of

the truck, they could hear country music blaring from inside.

"Hey, J," a pretty brunette cowgirl said as they walked through the door. "I haven't seen you for a while!" She led them upstairs to the table section where it was much quieter. "Do you want menus?"

Meghan looked at Jared, "You've told me about this delicious tenderloin here. I believe I want one of those with sweet iced tea."

"Make it the same for me."

"Be right back with your drinks," the waitress said with a smile.

"You just know everybody around here, don't you?"

"It's the perks of being a celebrity...and having roots here."

"So can I ask you a question?"

"Sure!"

"Why did you quit the rodeo?

"Well, most people around here probably knew about it if they remember it. It is a long, painful story that I don't share with too many new people that I meet, so you should be probably be feeling really special right about now."

"Okay...."

"Well...during the last rodeo I participated in, there was a little boy in the audience who wouldn't behave. His mother kept telling him to come back, to sit, to stay with her, stuff like that. Well, he wouldn't. They were making quite a spectacle of themselves in front of the crowd. People were really talking about them. She told him that if he didn't behave that they were going to have to leave, but the kid didn't quit, and they didn't leave. She told him that if he kept walking along where he was, he would fall in where the riders were. He kept on. Well, it was my turn to ride out; before we got on the bulls, we were supposed to make a lap or two around the arena on a horse; it was basically fanfare. As I first rode out around the ring, making the lap as the announcer was introducing me, I rode by where the kid was. He fell out into the arena just as I was riding by. It spooked my horse and the horse reared up and started to come down on the kid. I pulled at the reigns and jumped off so that I would hopefully cover the kid and take the brunt of the weight of the horse. However, it didn't quite work and the horse trampled the kid anyway. They rushed him to the hospital, but his injuries were too much. He died shortly after arriving there. His parents sued both the rodeo and me. People got really worked up when it was a child who was harmed. Some of them were even the ones who had been murmuring among each other about the child's defiant behavior when the mother couldn't or wouldn't control her child. However, when there is a child involved, everything seems to change. At the trial, however, there were a few witnesses who spoke about the child's behavior and the security camera footage was shown. The rodeo didn't have to pay any money but gave the child's parents a settlement as a goodwill gesture. I was found not responsible for the child's death, but in order to make a statement, the sponsors of the rodeo pulled their sponsorships from me, and I was deemed collateral damage for the rodeo. I was asked to never return to the rodeo due to the stigma I brought."

"But it wasn't your fault. You can't help it that the mom wouldn't make her kid mind. You can't help it just because you were riding right then. You did nothing wrong. You even tried to prevent it from happening."

"I know, but I still feel guilty for it."

"Why?"

"I don't know. People tend to place blame where it is the most convenient. Some people are jealous of others and are looking to blame them for something, anything. When enough people shun you and blame you, you start to lose your self-worth. Sometimes the guilt just overwhelms me."

The waitress came back with their tea.

"Thanks," they replied as she walked away.

"That was probably more than you wanted to hear," Jared said with eyes filling with tears.

"No, no. You need somebody to talk to sometimes."

"So... is there some big boyfriend who is going to hear about us being out here and come and beat me up?"

"Hardly!"

"So there isn't a boyfriend or he just isn't going to assault me?"

"No, neither," Meghan said, smiling. "You know it's kind of hard finding a guy who shares your values or isn't a total loser. Having a sick brother that you constantly have to be available to take care of isn't highly desirable either."

"That's too bad, but it's lucky for me, though," Jared said, grinning.

"Really...." Meghan smiled shyly. "I would have thought you would have found somebody to settle down with by now."

"No, I sure haven't." Jared's expression immediately turned to one of sadness, and he didn't offer any further explanation.

To patch the lull in the conversation, Meghan said, "So, tell me more about you. Not the stuff I can read in magazines or the internet, but the real you. I thought that you would be larger than life, but you seem so common, so normal. I haven't known you long, but at times you seem really preoccupied, like there is something really bothering you."

"Well, there is some behind the scenes stuff going on that not too many people know about."

"I saw you go into the lawyer's office yesterday when we went into town."

"Yes, that plays into all of this. It is a long story, but here it goes.... The home I live on is part of the original family homestead. The ranch next door was originally part of the family homestead, too. The entire family homestead belonged to my great-grandmother and great-grandfather. They had two children, my grandmother and her brother, my uncle, Leon. My uncle, who was significantly younger than my grandmother, always tried to weasel around and get whatever he wanted from his parents and his sister, and he usually got it done, too. When their parents eventually died, the huge ranch was divided into two smaller ranches, one for my grandmother and one for her brother. Leon was really mad that he didn't receive the entire parcel since he had gotten practically everything he ever wanted. Both he and my grandmother married people from around the area and then lived on their respective ranches. Leon was always trying to put a guilt trip on Grandmother, that he should have received the land since her husband's family had some land elsewhere, too. There was more than enough acreage on both of Leon's and Grandma's parallel parcels, but Leon is greedy and wanted it all. It turns out that the land was worth quite a bit of money. That fact made Leon want it all the more. Grandmother went on to have mom who eventually had me and then Sara. Leon went on to have a daughter, Maureen. Grandmother made up a will in which she willed the ranch so it would go to Mom when she died. However, in order for Mom to inherit it and keep it, there were stipulations. Mom had to remain living on this ranch. If she became incapable of living on this ranch or chose to move from it, the ranch would automatically go to Leon. When I was born, Grandma changed the will to include any of Mom's children but that it would go to us upon our mother's passing only if at least one of us were still unmarried and lived on and were able to take care of the ranch. If we decided to sell the ranch, it would automatically go to Leon. She wanted it to 'stay in the family.' We were not allowed to buy out each other's half either. She included all of these obstacles in hopes that we couldn't fulfill the requirements. That way it wouldn't be her fault that Leon got it. It would be that we didn't get it because we didn't want it bad enough to meet all of the requirements."

"Why didn't she just leave it to Leon if she wanted him to have it so badly?"

"She thought that people in town would talk bad about her. She cared what people said about her a little bit more than she cared about her brother."

"If your grandmother's parents left the land – divided in two – to both your grandmother and her brother, shouldn't his portion go to his descendants and hers go to you all?"

"Yes, that makes sense. However, Leon's greed and slyness and Grandma's gullibility played into it. It got worse when Leon lost his ranch to creditors because of his gambling debts. He came crying to grandma, who of course felt sorry for him and felt a responsibility to take care of her brother. Grandma seemed truly sorry that she had left the estate to us, thinking that she had abandoned Leon when he didn't have a roof over his head. It was his own fault, though. She probably would have drafted a new will leaving everything to Leon, but she died before she had time to think of it. She said she always wanted us to be able to stand on our own and not have much given to us. She didn't want us to be spoiled."

"That logic didn't seem to apply to Leon."

"It's always a double standard when it comes to him."

"Well what happened to Leon?"

"He lives in a small house in town. He seems to spend every cent he has now, when he isn't gambling it, trying to figure out how to get our land away from us. He seems to think that it is owed to him for some reason only he can figure out."

"Couldn't you just tear up the will?"

"She gave the original will to Leon for safekeeping, stating that he would do things right by us. She feared that we might tear it up so Leon wouldn't have had a chance at getting what shouldn't have been his. How ironic."

"Couldn't you fight it legally?

"We've tried pursuing it, but the county judge said it legally stands. We just have to do what it says if we wanted to inherit the property."

"Here are your tenderloins!" The waitress arrived with a plate for each of them. The tenderloin sandwich seemed to cover almost the entire plate and a side of fries so crispy, yet so soft, they practically melted as you chewed them.

"Wow! I've never tasted tenderloin this good!" Meghan exclaimed with her mouth full. "It's so good!"

The waitress grinned with great pleasure.

"I told her about them, but you really have to try it to understand," Jared said, putting the tenderloin sandwich up to his mouth, taking a bite.

"I can't believe you can have these everyday if you want them! Wow!" Meghan said after washing down the bite with a drink of sweet tea.

"Let me know if you need anything!" The waitress bounced off to check on another couple.

"What about your mother?" Meghan inquired.

"Well," Jared began, hitting the bottom of the upside down glass ketchup bottle with his hand. "She died recently." The ketchup began pouring all over his golden fries. "That's something else. Mom developed cancer. She wasn't feeling too well and eventually went to the doctor. He ran tests and found it – stage four liver cancer. Grandmother had already died, so mom called Leon to tell him. Instead of being sympathetic or trying to repair their relationship or even spend a little time with his sister before the end, Leon began legal proceedings to try to get the ranch. He thought that she would have to go to a nursing home, thus invoking the part of the will that says that mom has to live on the ranch or it becomes his. If she went to a care facility, he was going to try to get it because she wasn't deceased yet."

"How awful!" Meghan exclaimed.

"Yes, but we beat him at his game. We turned the tables on his plans. Sara is a registered nurse, and along with home health services, we took care of Mom at the ranch. Leon didn't consider that. A few months later Mom passed. Sara was divorced by then and had moved back to the ranch to take care of Mom; Sara's husband, a corporate guy, had found another, younger lady and left Sara and Tyler. I wasn't married, and I still lived on the ranch. When Sara found her husband and married, it was bittersweet. I wanted her to be happy and I was glad to eventually have a nephew, but in order to ensure us keeping the ranch, I knew then that I could never marry. That has been somewhat of a sore spot with me. "

"Couldn't you just move on and let Leon have the ranch?"

"Yes, we could, but I didn't want Leon to win. Grandma was always giving him money, so I didn't want him to get everything."

"Wow, there is a lot more to you than what one would read

about! Tyler said that his dad wants to spend more time with him now. How is Tyler taking all of it?"

"Well, he is a good kid. He can see what happened and whose fault it is. Tyler doesn't say much about it, but I can see that sometimes he is really hurting. He just kind of loses himself in his games, and Sid has been a good male role model for him; he's kind of taken him under his wing, so to speak."

"Yea, well you're a great role model for him, too."

"Well, I try."

"So, Sid seems to have really taken to my mom. He seems like such a fun-loving guy. What is his story?"

"Well, he is our cousin. When Leon began the 'feud,' he turned a bunch of the extended family against us. However, Sid never did like Leon; he could always see him for what he really was. Sid came out to the ranch one day and said that he thought that Leon was a crook and wanted to help us. Before all this, Sid and we were close; this only endeared him more to us. He moved in and has been the ranch hand ever since. He knew a lot about ranching because he had worked on another ranch for a while."

"Doesn't he have any family?"

"His wife died when they were pretty young. They couldn't have children. I don't know that he ever really got over all of that, and I don't see how he can be so positive all the time. However, he loves children – probably because he couldn't have any – so it has been a blessing to have him around, especially for Tyler."

"So, is there more about the Leon situation?"

"Yes, well, when Sara's divorce finalized, Leon was at it again. He sicked his lawyer on us again, saying that Grandma's will had read that we had to be unmarried and be able to take care of the ranch."

"Yes, neither of you were married."

"He said that since Sara had been married, that it counted. The county judge ruled with him on that."

"Yes, but you weren't...were you?"

"No, but it said that you had to be able to take care of the ranch. I ended up in the hospital a few weeks ago. I thought that

I was having a heart attack, but it turned out to be stress from all that has been going on. Leon caught wind that I was in the hospital and is trying to make the case that I cannot take care of the ranch. We can get hired help, but the will reads so that I have to be in shape to take care of it. That's what Sara and I were talking about the other night in the office – about having to contact Larry – and why I had to go to the lawyer's office the next day. Leon has subpoenaed my medical records, trying to prove me unfit to run a ranch."

"It is so beautiful; you shouldn't lose it to Leon. That's so unfair. There is no reason that it should be his."

"I know. But the county judge hates us. Back in the day, he was in love with mom. They dated a little bit, and he really had feelings for her. She just didn't think that they were compatible, especially when he showed his true colors of how vindictive and cruel he could really be. When she broke up with him and eventually married Dad, the judge wanted to do everything in his power to hurt her and get back at her and us."

"But it wasn't your fault about their past."

"Tell him! He is the one who presided over lawsuit that the parents of the kid at the rodeo brought against the rodeo and me. He couldn't realistically find me responsible any more than the rodeo itself. However, he presided over the civil suit that the family of the kid that I hurt and killed at the rodeo brought against me. He found me guilty of negligence and hoped to bankrupt me with the judgement settlement. He thought that I would have had to ask Mom to mortgage the ranch, but I had the cash in reserve. Leon was already offering to buy the ranch to help us out."

"But he didn't have the money."

"He would have borrowed for it; then it could have been foreclosed upon. If he couldn't have it, he wanted to make sure that we weren't going to."

"Couldn't you have appealed the decision?"

"Sure, but it probably would have cost more in the end, and people were really up in arms about the kid. It probably would have cost more than it would have been worth. It's hard to legally clear your name and even harder to clear your name in people's minds."

"Wow. This could be a reality show."

"I know!"

By then, they had eaten about half of their meals.

"Wow, I am so full!"

"Me, too!"

"How about some more tea and some dessert, y'all?" The waitress approached with the pitcher of tea.

"Oh, no, not for me," Meghan exhaled, proving she was completely filled.

"They have great apple cobbler...." Jared laughed.

"No can do!"

"Why don't you put our leftovers in a to-go box and throw in a piece of cobbler for each of us for later?" Jared politely asked the waitress. "Can you put it in the fridge?"

"Sure thing!"

"What's going on?" Meghan questioned with a turn of her head and a gleam in her eye.

"We're going dancing! Downstairs, remember the music? It will help lighten the mood from old Uncle Leon. Plus, with all of this exercise, you won't have to do your workout videos tonight."

They could hear the beat of the music getting louder the farther they went downstairs. People had just lined up for a country line dance. Meghan grabbed Jared's hand and pulled him into the line. It turned out that Meghan and Jared were both really good dancers. The song seemed to never end. However, as the song finally ended, both Meghan and Jared were laughing, a little out of breath. The song changed to a slow country song. Both of them kind of paused, looking down and shuffling their feet for a moment. Then, as if in the same rhythmic motion, both looked at each other and automatically began to come together for a slow dance. With her arms wrapped around his neck, and his arms draped around her waist, they moved in motion with the song. In that moment, it felt as though they were meant for each other. They were puzzle pieces coming together to create a magnificent larger work of art. Meghan was just a few inches shorter than Jared, she noticed, as she gazed up into his soft brown eyes. She then laid her head against his shoulder, feeling the softness of his shirt, and realizing that she had never been this happy in her life. Jared realized that he even though he had dated some, and at rodeos, women had practically thrown themselves at him, offers which he never accepted, he had never really found "the one." Oh, at times, he had wondered if a certain person was "the one," but it never seemed to work out. He wanted someone who shared his values and beliefs and was hopefully kind of pretty, too! He wanted someone who could complete him. He could feel the warmth radiating from Meghan's head on his shoulder as they danced under the warmth of the lights from the disc jockey. Could she be the one?

As they drove home from their date, Jared slipped his arm around Meghan, who again was sitting next to him in the truck. She smiled and snuggled in. The next day would be Sunday. After church, Meghan and her family were going to be heading home. The few days had flown by faster than either one of them had anticipated. Now each of them would be going back to their "normal" lives. What had started as a mission to help a young man had turned into the beginning of a romance that neither of them had seen coming. It was true that they were living only five hours apart, but in the scope of all the impacting events in their lives, they might as well be living light years apart. Could a long distance relationship work? If Jared married, he and his family stood to lose everything. Would he be willing to give up everything for her? Would she be able to leave her mother and brother to start a life all her own again? Who was she kidding? She knew that she couldn't leave her brother now. How could she even think about her life beyond his? How could she have such selfish thoughts? Could Jared comfort her in the grief she knew would come? Though it was a slow, quiet ride back to Jared's, their thoughts raced out of control.

That evening, after most everyone had gone to bed, Jared was sitting at his desk in his office. Papers and folders were strewn haphazardly across his desk. As he was hanging up his telephone, he heard a light tap on the door, and there stood Meghan with a warm smile. She came in. "I'm missing being here already."

"I'm missing having you all around."

"I wanted to thank you for tonight and all that you did for my brother. I don't know how long he will live, but this has been the best few days that he has ever had or will ever have. You don't know how much it has meant to me to be here...and to spend time with you."

Jared got up and stepped closer, bending his head close to hers. Her lips rose to meet his. It was a simple, warm kiss, not passionate like in the movies. She pulled her head back, her eyes filled with tears. She looked down at the floor, then gently, slowly patted his chest and turned around, running back to her room.

CHAPTER
6

When Meghan rose the next morning, she hoped to catch Jared before seeing the others and apologize for her emotional state the prior evening. She had been having a whirlwind of emotions – happiness, grief, sadness, love – all in the last few days and sometimes all intertwining at the same time. She had never felt the way she felt now; she was in love with someone whom she might never see again; the problem was that she didn't know for sure how he felt about her. What had the kiss last night meant?

When she came into the kitchen, she noticed that everyone but Jared was gathered around the table, feasting on crispy bacon and lightly scrambled eggs. As she sat down and began filling her plate, she couldn't help but wonder where Jared was, and more importantly, if he was avoiding her.

As they were loading up to go to church, Sid said that Jared wouldn't be attending with them. Something had come up that he had to attend to. Later, no matter how hard she tried, Meghan couldn't seem to concentrate on the sermon. Her mind kept wandering back to Jared and if she had done something to cause him to distance himself the morning after their date and subsequent kiss.

After they returned from church, they all gathered outside for cold cuts and potato salad. Eventually, Jared quietly slipped back into the backyard and grabbed a chair next to Johnny. Meghan gave Jared a questioning look, which seemed to be lost on him; Jared was bent over, whispering something to Johnny who, in turn, grinned and nodded his head.

After they finished eating, Jared announced, "Well, I believe that Johnny has something he would like to show you...."

Johnny went running to the stables with everyone quickly following. Jared helped Johnny onto his pony and then mounted his own. "Okay, everyone, Johnny wants to show you his riding skills!"

At this, they both took off at a slow trot, with Jared guiding the small pony Johnny was riding. After a couple times around the pasture, Johnny was met with a huge cry of jubilation from everyone. There wasn't a dry eye in the group as Johnny kept exclaiming, "Look, everybody, I did it. I'm actually riding!"

After pictures and videos were taken and uploaded to social media, it was time for everyone to say their goodbyes. Hugs and handshakes were shared with Johnny lingering extra-long with Jared. "I don't wanna go. It just isn't fair."

"I know...but you'll have to remember all of these good times and plan for more to come," Jared said, bending down to Johnny's level and wiping a tear from Johnny's eye. "You've gotten to do a lot more already than a lot of fellers your age. You've learned to ride, and more importantly, you got to meet Jared 'Bronc Buster' Cochran!"

Meghan couldn't help but admire how good Jared was with Johnny. Momentarily, Jared stood up and put his arms out to her. She met his embrace, and he whispered, "I'll never forget you."

She nodded, not willing to let herself speak. Turning around she put her arm around Johnny and guided him to the limousine that had been parked in front of the house. Sid was gathering their luggage and placing it into the trunk.

Again, not a dry eye was found in either group as the limo pulled away.

As the group in the limousine started the long drive back, Sid and Jennifer kept up a steady stream of conversation. Johnny kept talking to whomever would listen about his learning to ride and his getting to meet Jared "Bronc Buster" Cochran. Though she was among those whom she had known her entire life, Meghan had never felt so alone. She could see her entire future becoming more and more distant as the limousine pulled farther and farther away. Would she ever see Jared again? Was she reading more into this than there could ever be? She hadn't known him very long, but it seemed like there was an instant connection made, a connection she didn't want broken.

CHAPTER
7

Work in the vet's office Monday seemed so mundane as Meghan assisted the veterinarian with declawing a stray cat who had recently been adopted by a loving family.

"What's wrong, girl?" her friend Abby, the receptionist, asked Meghan she came out of the examination room.

"Nothing."

"I know you too well. This is not nothing."

"I really don't want to talk about it."

"Okay, but you know I'm here for when you do."

Meghan periodically checked her phone for missed calls or messages. Nothing. She thought that what she and Jared had, or at least what she thought that they had, was real. Why wouldn't he call her or text her? A sharp pang of anxiety shot through her. Who was she kidding? He would no doubt forget her soon. He was a celebrity, and she was just a country bumpkin. A nobody.

Two days later, after returning home and preparing for bed, Meghan eventually checked her phone. She noticed that there was one missed call with a message awaiting her in her cell phone inbox. She quickly pushed the button and heard Jared's voice, sounding strained and a bit far away; maybe it was just bad reception during the recording. He said slowly, "Meghan, sorry I didn't call you before…. Something came up, but I just wanted to say how much I enjoyed the past few days with you and that I…." The message ended at this point. That was it? Seriously!

"Something always seems to come up, doesn't it," she thought, seething with anger. Why did he wait so long to call? What could have been so important? She decided that she wasn't going to call him back. She shut off her phone and angrily went to bed.

"Meghan, wake up!" Jennifer urgently shook her daughter. "Wake up!" Tears were pouring down Jennifer's face.

"Mom, what's the matter? Has something happened to Johnny?"

"It isn't Johnny, honey…. It's Jared."

"Jared?"

"Yes, honey, he died."

CHAPTER
8

"What?"

"I don't know what happened, but Sid found your number in Jared's phone and has been trying to get ahold of you all late last night and early this morning. He couldn't get you to answer, so he called information and finally got our landline number. Honey, hurry and get dressed; we've got to get back to northern Missouri immediately."

This was the fastest that any family had ever packed and left. Meghan felt an emptiness in her as her mother drove them in her SUV. They had waited to tell Johnny the news until they were travelling. He broke down, wailing inconsolably, just as they had suspected he would. His wailing only served to cover Meghan's own desperate sobbing.

Without any bathroom breaks along the way, Jennifer pulled up the lane to the ranch in record time. Sid, with tears streaming down his face, met them outside with arms wide open. It was then that Jennifer finally broke down, letting Sid hold her as they both cried.

They eventually made their way inside the house and sat down in the living room. It seemed like there was a vast emptiness present without Jared sitting alongside them.

"What happened?" Meghan cried.

"Well," began Sid, "Saturday night, after you all got back from your date, Meghan, Leon's lawyer called. Leon had a massive stroke earlier in the week and eventually decided that he desperately wanted to talk to Jared by Saturday night or early Sunday morning." Meghan realized that was who Jared had been on the phone with when she came to his office Saturday night. "Well, they weren't sure how long Leon was going to last by the end of the week, so Jared went to the hospital early Sunday morning, as Leon and his lawyer had asked. Leon had finally realized how awful he had acted all along. He had been so awful that his own daughter and her family wouldn't even visit him in the hospital. After that week of being scared and alone in the hospital, he realized the mistakes that he had made all along. Even though Leon had turned family against us, they still didn't want to be around him. The only one to visit him was the hospital chaplain. They had a long talk about his life. He had the nurse to call in his lawyer and draft a legal document that said, in short, he was ashamed of the way that he had acted all of these years. He knew that he couldn't make the past right, but he wanted to do what he could to make up for the way that he had acted. He wanted to call off the 'feud,' and he would no longer pursue getting the ranch in any way. He explained all of this to Jared then – he had been thinking and working on this for most of the week. Then, they gave Jared the new legal document along with the original will that their grandmother had given Leon. Leon's lawyer left, and then Jared and Leon had a long talk afterward. Nobody knows what was said. Leon had another massive stroke Sunday night and died the early Monday morning."

"But what about Jared?" cried Meghan.

"After you all left on Sunday, Jared went to town for a while, and when he returned home, he started getting sick. He wouldn't admit it, but I could tell. I had the ambulance to come and get him. He was in the hospital Monday and Tuesday. He didn't want us to call you all; he said that you all had enough to worry about as it was. That he would be fine. The hospital determined that he hadn't had a heart attack – just another episode of stress. He thought that the stress would pass since the issues with Leon had come to an end. It was just such a shock that Leon had turned over a new leaf, per se. However, lifetime stress had taken its toll on J. When Jared came back to the ranch early Wednesday, he spent some time alone in his office, writing something and then rode out with his collie to the upper pasture. He refused to rest, saying he had to stay busy and needed to think about his future. He seemed to do his best thinking working on the barbed wire. I hadn't seen him for a while, and then the collie came back to the house here and tried to get me to go with him. I rode out to check on J. I found him slumped over against the fencepost, with his phone still in his hand. I thought maybe he was trying to dial for help, but I saw the last phone call he had made was to you, Miss Meghan. It seemed like he was trying to record a message and then just keeled over, dead. I called the ambulance but they couldn't revive him. This time it was more than stress – it was a massive heart attack. Meghan, he really loved you." Tears began streaming down Sid's face.

Meghan burst into tears. The border collie that had been forlornly laying on the ground next to J's big, stuffed chair, jumped up onto the couch and put his head on Meghan's lap.

"I hope you all can stay for the funeral. Though we didn't know you until only a few days ago, you are like family now, and I can't imagine going through this without you all now," Sid continued.

"We sure will. I'll call and rearrange our schedules," Jennifer replied.

That night, Meghan, for the first time since Johnny's cancer diagnosis, cried herself to sleep.

CHAPTER
9

The day of Jared's funeral was gloomy, in both the weather and the attitudes of the attendees. Since Jared had reached celebrity status in life, all of the major news networks had played endless footage of his career when they received word of his passing. Those who had spoken harsh words about Jared or who had completely ignored him over the past few years, including family and people who were interviewed on the news, now spoke of him as if he had been their best friend, favorite relative, and most beloved celebrity to ever live. All stations wanted to broadcast the funeral, but Sara declined the offers and chose instead to have a private graveside service for close family and friends only. She wanted those who were truly hurting to be able to grieve together in private and not be interrupted by those who only wanted to ostentatiously "perform" during the service. Each of Jared's close family and friends, along with the family minister, took a turn speaking of Jared's influence on their lives. Sid spoke of how Jared took him in and kept him on, working on the ranch. Tyler cried and said that Jared was the best uncle a boy could ask for. Sara even tearfully said that she knew that Jared had ignored the chance at finding happiness so that she could go on with her life and the family ranch would still remain theirs. He had sacrificed so that she could go ahead and marry, start a family, and always be guaranteed of having a roof over their heads if times became tough.

After the grave side services, they all returned to the ranch where they had a catered meal of Jared's favorites – tenderloins and fries – as a celebration of life for Jared. After everyone else had left, Sara, Tyler, Sid, Jennifer, Meghan, and Johnny joined

Jared's lawyer in the family room. Though Jennifer, Meghan, and Johnny tried to leave and let the family begin the legal work, Jared's lawyer insisted that they stay.

The lawyer began, "As you know I was not only Jared's attorney, but also his friend. I, too, grieve with you today, but I know that Jared is in a better place, and all things here will be taken care of according to his wishes. I knew that Jared had not been feeling well, and on Sunday, after the Schulte family left from their visit to the ranch, he met with me. Jared had just spent time with his uncle, Leon, that morning. Nobody knows for sure what all was said, but Leon gave up his claim on the pursuit of this ranch. His lawyer gave Jared the paperwork, including the original will, and then left them to talk alone. I personally think that Jared then realized how short and how precious life really is. Having this new found legal freedom allowed Jared to make some new decisions about the future. He spoke with Sara first and then met with me. We drew up some legal paperwork later on Sunday afternoon, right before Jared had to be rushed to the hospital. In short, the following are the details. Since Tyler's dad wants to be more of a part of Tyler's life, Sara has been wanting to move closer to where he lives now. She has recently been looking for homes and hospital or clinic jobs in the St. Louis area. Last week, she found the perfect home after being offered a job there at a local hospital; she never loved the ranch like Jared did. She knew that Jared wanted to keep the ranch, at least in part, so that she would always have a roof over her head. It was especially important since her divorce. She also didn't want to leave Jared here, responsible for taking care of the ranch, which is half hers. Remember that according to your grandmother's will, it couldn't be sold or it would be forfeited to Leon. Therefore, Jared couldn't buy her out, and she didn't have enough money to afford two residences. But, since Leon dropped the legal issues Sunday morning, Jared drew up new legal paperwork with me. He paid Sara, buying out her part of the ranch. With the money that she already had and the money for her half, she will have a nice amount to settle in her new home near St. Louis. Jared also made a will Sunday night that if anything should happen to him, the ranch will go to Sid. He has worked on it for years, and he considers it home. Finally, Jared made plans to give $300,000 to the Schulte family for Johnny's past, present, and future medical expenses and for Meghan's schooling. This means that he wants Johnny to have a transplant, if he is physically able, even if the insurance won't pay for it. The rest of the money will be to help pay for medical expenses already accrued and for Meghan's veterinary school tuition."

"I don't know what to say..." Jennifer exclaimed.

The lawyer walked over to Meghan, with her mouth still gaping open, and handed her an envelope. "Jared was going to send this to you. Since he cannot, I wanted to give it to you now. I have no idea what the contents are."

As they dispersed from the meeting, each went back to his or her room, still in shock, to pack to return home. Meghan had already packed most of her stuff, so she sat down and with her thumb, slit open the sealed envelope. Tears filled her eyes as she read:

My Dearest Meghan,

I am not a deep, philosophical thinker. I had so many things I wanted to say to you but was unable to do so. I am sitting down right after you left to compose this letter. Maybe it will be easier in writing than by saying these things to you.

First, I have fallen in love with you. I have always put others ahead of me and never pursued and found true happiness, but I feel that with you I have. I feel that we could have a good future together. I am not one to jump into anything, but I would appreciate it if you would keep an open mind about eventually marrying me. You are beautiful both externally and internally. You, too, have put others ahead of you, and you deserve happiness.

Second, I am sorry that I was unable to spend more time with you earlier today. Leon and his lawyer asked for me to come by the hospital. Nobody else would come and see him; he's been too mean throughout his life. He talked to the hospital chaplain who helped him make some decisions about his eternal future. He also felt that he needed to make right some things that he had done. After his lawyer gave me the paperwork and left, and we were alone, Leon and I began the process of "mending fences." When he asked for my forgiveness, it wasn't like in some books or movies where he and I embraced and I cried, "I forgive you" with tears streaming down my face. I told him that I appreciated his gesture, but he had done too much for too long. Actions have consequences. I would take into consideration what he had just said and done, but it was going to take a lot of time to forgive all of those years and everything he had done. I don't want strife and discord, so I said that I would pray for help to forgive him. That's all I could do. I have been praying that God will help me to forgive Leon and Grandma, too, and I am beginning the healing process. Contrary to what others like to say, it takes time to heal. Also, you helped me to realize that I truly am not responsible for the boy's death at the rodeo no matter what others may think or who they try to blame. I have come to terms with this and am at peace with all things.

Third, I am giving you all $300,000 for medical expenses and for you to attend veterinary school. You may think that I helped change your lives, but I am truly the one whose life has been changed. I have found the meaning of the words "friends" and "family." I have also fallen in love.

Please consider a future with me.

Love,

Jared

CHAPTER
10

Five years later...

Meghan was just a couple of minutes away from her turnoff. She was returning to the Circle C Ranch. As she pulled up the lane, the border collie came running down to meet her truck and chase her all the way to the house. When she parked and got out, the dog jumped up and started giving her lots of "kisses."

Sid came out of the house with Jennifer right behind him. A couple of years of courtship had led him to proposing, her to accepting, and her to moving to the ranch. Meghan heard a noise behind her. A school bus had pulled up at the end of the lane. The bus driver, a heavy set looking man with a brown scraggly beard, opened the doors and then waved at them as he pulled away. The border collie went running down the lane to meet Johnny, now fifteen.

"Meggie!" Johnny yelled, running toward her. "You're here! Guess what! In another year, I'll be able to drive myself to school and to get cheeseburgers, and to come visit you!"

They embraced and then headed into the house.

Meghan stayed for a couple of days, and as she was leaving town, she stopped by the cemetery. She walked to the tombstone of the man she loved. She placed fresh flowers in the vase and began a conversation. "I know that you can't hear me. Only your body is here, but I want to talk. The money you left us more than paid for everything. I'm a vet now. I just graduated from school, and I am going to be practicing where I have been working all these years. Your sister is just finishing medical school. Tyler's dad and she got back together, and I went to their wedding. Tyler is going to have a sister soon. Johnny's doing great. The transplant was expensive, but it seemed to be exactly what he needed. He's in remission. We don't know for how long, but you're right, each day is a blessing. Oh, and he's going to be driving next year. Sid is going to teach him. You would be so proud of him. Mom and Sid have been great for each other. They're a quirky pair. Well, I don't know how to say this, but I met somebody. He's in medical school, finishing his residency. I think you would really like him. He has gone on summer mission trips to help third-world countries. He's not you. Nobody will ever be you. I don't know where this will lead, but I just had to come by and said that we're all doing okay. I have been coming to terms with my dad's death, my brother's sickness, and your death. I've been trying to forgive whoever I need to and go on. I now understand why you loved to work with barbed wire in the north pasture. I now understand what you meant about praying to forgive Leon. I now understand mended fences."

ABOUT THE AUTHOR

Brian J. Hill has been a high school and college English and Speech teacher in Missouri for the last fifteen years. He holds both a B.S. Ed. in English and an MA in English. He has additionally reviewed college texts for publication.

Made in the USA
Las Vegas, NV
11 November 2021